To Auggie
Christmas .
Merry
Stanley E. Wilcinski

The Christmas That Almost Never Was

Stanley E. Wiklinski

Art by Gary A. Lippincott

Lost in the year of the great blizzard blow
Found preserved in the deep Polar snow
Here's the tale creating the buzz
of the Christmas that almost never was

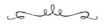

Jabberwocky Books
2301 Lucien Way #415
Maitland, FL 32751
407.339.4217
www.jabberwocky-books.com

Jabberwocky
Books

Printed in the United States of America

ISBN-13: 978-0-99986-240-7
LCCN: 2018902254

DEDICATION

To my dear wife, Barbara Ann, you have given me a lifetime of beauty, love, and adventure – and four beautiful children!

ACKNOWLEDGEMENTS

Please know, each of you, my appreciation and gratitude to you. Each one of <u>you</u> played a part in bringing *The Christmas That Almost Never Was,* to life:

Jim and Nancy Fay
Keith Cartnick
Ed Welch, Esq,
Gary Lippincott
Henry Winkler
Chic Ciccolini
Dominic Rossetti
Bob Ross
Peter Hanson
Dan Van Winkle
Janice Onken
Lauren Pashuk
Linda Sayers Sandrey
Ellen Anderson Angelique
Christine Fahey

Joan Berg Victor
Joe and Nancy Sendek
Charles and Peggy Brooks
Linc and Chip Mueller
Tom and Mary Keifer
Chandra Thomas
Benjamin Seyler
Krystle Prashad
Michelle Brown
Our children:
    Stanley
    Stephen
    Jennifer
    Melissa

Dr. Louis Cartnick, my dear Father-in-Law and
Mrs. Frances Mildred Cartnick my dear Mother-in-Law

And all the wonderful people who made this project a reality by donating through "gofundme"

A half-moon shone in the
Polar sky,
Like a warm and friendly
winking eye.
The North Star twinkled
with delight,
A diamond sparkling in
the night.
And far below in the hollow
of a hill,
Nestled snug lay Santaville.

Down the streets and winding lanes,
Candles glowed through frosty panes,
While inside sounds of joy and laughter
Echoed from each floor and rafter.
Piles of gifts and toys increasing
Santa's workers never ceasing,

Helpers crowded every table,
Fingers flying quick and able,
Sawing, shaping, painting, sewing,
Trains and dolls and boats for rowing.
Sugar treats in candy boxes,
Cuddly bears and slinky foxes.
With needles, hammers, saws and blade,
A thousand dreams were being made.

The village clock with snowcapped tower,
Bonged the lonely midnight hour.
With drooping eyes and nodding heads,
Santa's helpers trudged to their beds.
Tomorrow's work till dawn would keep.
Santaville was soon asleep.

It struck without warning in the deep of the night, and
Hurled through the village with fury and might.
With a swoop came the snow, with a boom the wind's shout,
And a wild, gusting blizzard blew the moon out!
It swelled without ceasing, it ripped through the morn,
It raced down the streets, howling, forlorn.
Higher and higher the drifting snow reared,
And little by little, the town disappeared.

The doors to the stable, where the reindeer lay,
Had come unhinged and were blown away.
Through the long and raging storm-tossed night,
The reindeer huddled in terrible fright.
Then it began, the sniffles and sneezing;
The stable soon shook with coughing and wheezing.

Santa called to Tweeter, who tended the stable,
"Hurry, Tweeter, go get Dr. Able!"
Veterinarian Able, a doctor who cared,
A total professional, always prepared,
Arrived in an instant and knew what to do.
A thousand such crises he had been through!

One by one, he examined their throats,
Shook his head in dismay, made voluminous notes.
He looked at their eyes, all brimming and puffy;
He'd never seen noses so runny and stuffy.
He tapped on their chests, he thumped on their backs,
He patiently paused through their sneezing attacks.
At long last he said, as he let out a sigh,
"They've all got the flu, Santa. The reindeer can't fly."

This was calamity! This was a fix!
This was an earth-shaking mess of a mix!
In panic and fear, the village was caught.
Santa alone sat calmly and thought.
When he arose, all eyes on him lay;
All waited to hear what he had to say.

"Be quick, everyone! There's no time to waste!
Load our bus with the reindeer; we've got to make haste.
Bring Dasher and Dancer, bring Prancer and Vixen,
Bring Comet and Cupid and Dunder and Blitzen.
Bundle them warm, wrap each in a shawl,
And follow me, follow me, follow me, all!"

Up rose a tumult, a great joyous shout.
Santaville's tower bells pealed and rang out.
In an instant, the villagers lost all their fears.
They rushed to assemble with streamers and cheers!
There was joy in their cheering and joy in their manner.
With shouts, they unfurled the Santaville banner!

"Let's go!" shouted Santa as he held up his hand,
And off they stepped into that cold, frozen land.
Through daylight dimming on the drifting snow,
Through graying twilight's misty glow,
Past gloomy mountains, ghostly white,
The pilgrims trudged into the night.

The light of dawn rose swift and clean,
The sky a blush of tangerine.
Santa, nearing the crest of a hill,
Wheeled and whispered, "Shhh! Be still!"
Step by careful step, he went
The last few yards of the ascent.

Then from his lips escaped a cheer.
He whirled and said, "They're here! They're here!"
The villagers gasped in amazement and awe
At the utter fantastic sight that they saw:
Polar bears here, Polar bears there,
Polar bears jumping high in the air!

In great arching leaps, they spiraled and rolled,
Then tucked into flips that were daring and bold.
They roared in for landings, abandoned of care,
Then hurled themselves again in the air.
They glided, they planed; it was awesome, tremendous,
A mind-boggling air show that was simply stupendous!

Santa threw up his arms and called them by name,
And, hearing his voice, they immediately came!
What a joyous reunion, wild and dramatic.
The bears, seeing Santa, were simply ecstatic!
Santa kept saying, "What a sight for sore eyes!
Why, you're all so grown up; just look at your size!"

Santa continued. "Here's why I am here:
Without your help, there will be no Christmas this year.
This Christmas, my friends, is all up to you.
My reindeer can't take me; they've all got the flu!"

Pauline, the Polar bear with petal-blue eyes,
Who knew every star that studded the skies,
Said, "Santa, we know we jump very high,
But we've never, ever been able to fly!"

Then up piped the reindeer, all talking as one,
"In all of this world, there's no greater fun;
The moment you'll fly is when you believe it.
We'll do all we can to help you achieve it!"

Pauline, whose bright eyes shone with a gleam,
And six other bears completed a team.
Snowdrift and Jumper, Puller and Cloud,
Stormy and Glacier were all very proud.

A ski jump was built from the top of a hill.
A crowd had assembled, waiting breathless and still.

Oh how many times, and oh how they tried,
Careening headlong down that perilous slide
To be vaulted each time high in the air
Only to crash to the earth in despair.
The bears were magnificent when jumping alone,
But trying together, they all fell like stone!

"Oh, yes!" shouted Santa as he leapt into the air.
"I know what's missing: the spirit's not there!
They've really been trying with a lot of desire,
But we've got to give them some fuel for their fire!"

The crowd began to chant and cheer,
"Try! Try! Try! Try!
Fly! Fly! Fly! Fly!
High! High! High! High!"

Up climbed the bears with unrestrained pride.
They bristled with grit at the top of the slide.
Every muscle was taught, every sinew and bone;
They were poised, they were ready, and they weren't alone!

Down they came in a mad, roaring sound
As wild cheers burst from the crowd on the ground.
Plummeting down, in seconds they gained
The thundering speed of a runaway train.
Faster, still faster, their flashing legs flew
As the crowd, nearing frenzy, still wilder grew!

Pandemonium broke; there was screaming and hailing!
The bears vaulted up and up and just kept on sailing!
'Round and 'round in great circles they flew
With Pauline proudly leading her crew.
Puller, Stormy, Glacier, and Cloud,
Snowdrift and Jumper turned earthward and bowed!

It came at last, it was Christmas Eve,
Santa and the bears were soon to leave.
The night was calm, the moon was high,
The reindeer standing sadly by.
Every villager had come,
Santa thanked them, every one.

He walked to where the reindeer stood,
And, one by one, as best he could,
He whispered in each reindeer's ear
Words that only they could hear.
Then swiftly climbed into his sleigh;
It seemed he brushed a tear away.

The bears were pawing at the snow,
Straining forward, set to go.
Santa snapped, "Now, ready all!
Listen up and heed my call!"
His voice was booming, sharp, and clear.
"Tonight by starlight will we steer!"

"Now up, Pauline! Up, Puller! Up, Stormy! Up, Cloud!
You, Snowdrift! There, Jumper! You, Glacier;
look proud!"
With sweeping force, he raised his hand.
They leaped at once to his command,
And silent as a bird in flight,
They rose as one into the night.

All below heard Santa say,
In crystal words that trailed away...

"Santa comes on Christmas Eve
To all good children who believe!"

Stanley E. Wiklinski has an MFA from the Yale University, School of Drama. Following graduation from Yale, he acted on Broadway, as well as for regional theater and television. He is, as well, a retired United States Navy Reserve Commander. He is married with four children and five grandchildren. *The Christmas That Almost Never Was* is his debut children's book.

Gary Lippincott has been going to work on the back of a dragon for many years. His delicate, highly detailed watercolors have graced the covers of books, illustrated stories, hung in galleries, and been purchased by collectors worldwide. He lives in the "wild" of Massachusetts and considers himself extremely fortunate to do what he does for a living.